Welcome to the Kingdom of Zork!

You are bored. There's nothing on TV except some stupid reruns. You wander into your local book store and pick up an interesting-looking book entitled *Zork: The Malifestro Quest.* As usual, you turn to the first page and begin reading.

The book is set in the magical land of Zork, where the evil and greedy wizard Malifestro has imprisoned Syovar, the rightful ruler of the kingdom, and only YOU can save the day! There are elves, trolls, magic potions, a flying carpet, the Snow Monster of Snurth, and a giant empire to explore. It looks like this book is good!

Do you choose to save the kingdom? If so, purchase the book and turn to page 7.

Or do you choose to go home and watch reruns? Turn to the next page.

In front of the TV, your eyelids slowly close. A strange sound fills the room. Suddenly your eyes open; you realize that you have been snoring.

You can't get that Zork book out of your mind, but the bookstore is already closed.

Think again! Wouldn't it be wise to purchase the book now, and turn to page 5?

#2

THE MALIFESTRO QUEST

S. ERIC MERETZKY

A TOM DOHERTY ASSOCIATES BOOK

This is a work of fiction. All the characters and events portrayed in this book are fictional, and any resemblance to real people or incidents is purely coincidental.

A Tor Book

Published by Tom Doherty Associates, 8-10 W. 36th St., New York, New York 10018

First printing, September 1983

ISBN: 0-812-57980-1

Printed in the United States of America

Distributed by Pinnacle Books, 1430 Broadway, New York, New York 10018

6

The room is oppressively hot, and dimly lit by a few tiny windows set high in the walls. A hissing, writhing mass of snakes covers the entire floor.

Syovar hangs from a rope tied securely to his hands. He is suspended only a foot or so above the ground. Sweat pours down his face as snakes hiss and snap at his feet.

Syovar gives a moan of pain. His lips do not move but, somehow, he seems to be speaking:

"Come. . . . Take the ancient underground route. . . . Seek the black crystal sphere. . . . Hurry. . . ."

His words fade away, and are replaced by a distant pounding. It seems to come from everywhere. The pounding grows louder and louder. . . .

Bill awakens from his nightmare with a start. He sits up in bed, shaking, and tries to get his bearings. He remembers that it is Saturday, the first day of summer vacation. Sunlight is streaming into his bedroom. He realizes that the pounding from his dream is still going on. It comes from the direction of his window. He looks over and sees June outside, banging on the window.

Turn to page 8.

Bill opens the window and June climbs in. She appears to have dressed in a hurry, and is very out of breath.

"I just had a horrible dream," she pants. "Syovar was in trouble. He was calling for us. We. . . ."

"I just had a dream exactly like that, too!" Bill interrupts.

Both Bill and June feel guilty. They had adventured through the Land of Zork before. There they had been given the Zorkish names, "Bivotar" and "Juranda," and had been pronounced heroes by their mysterious "uncle," Syovar. They had vowed to return soon to that magical land.

But as Bill and June and their friends made plans for the vacation ahead, thoughts of adventuring faded like the snows of winter.

Now comes this jolting reminder of that other world. Bill opens the top drawer of his chest and removes the Ring of Zork, their gift from Syovar. The ring is pulsing with flashes of vivid light.

"Bill, this can't be a coincidence! The dreams, the ring—we're being summoned for some important reason. Let's go!"

Go to page 9.

"But I haven't had breakfast yet. . . ."

"Forget about breakfast! Syovar is in trouble."

Bill stares at the flashing ring, beckoning them toward another adventure. Holding June with one hand, he slowly slips the Ring of Zork onto his finger.

With a flash of light and a puff of heavy smoke, they find themselves in a bedroom—but a very different one. This room is large with a very high ceiling, and it is dead silent.

Turn to page 10.

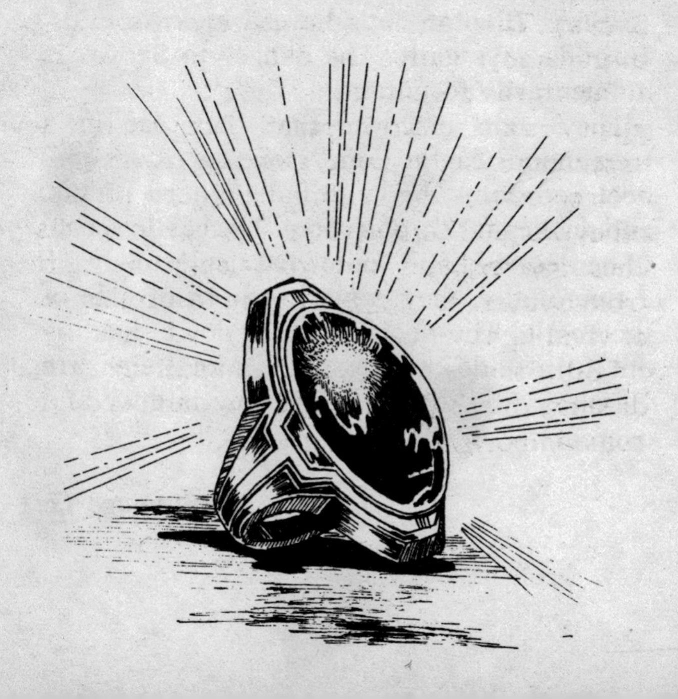

The walls and floors are of polished stone. The bed is large and covered by a woven canopy. A massive oak door, lying open, leads out to a dim corridor. A dead silence pervades the room.

Their clothes have changed also. They are now dressed in adventurers' garb, featuring leather belts, hooded cloaks, and sturdy leather boots. They are now Bivotar and Juranda.

"Well, Juranda, should we look around?" He feels the excitement of adventuring returning.

"Sure, Bivotar, let's have a look around." Juranda says gaily. The danger to Syovar is momentarily forgotten.

They soon discover that they are in a tremendous castle. Long, stone corridors connect bedrooms, banquet halls, guard rooms, and an elegant throne room. The castle seems to be deserted and somewhat neglected.

Eventually, they come to the front gate of the castle. The drawbridge is down, leading out to a wide, grassy plain. Mountains are visible in the distance. The day is gray and overcast.

Turn to page 12.

Across from the gate, a forbidding doorway leads into a darkened room. Several large rats scurry among some skulls and bones scattered near the door.

"What should we do, Biv?" Juranda asks. "The castle looks deserted."

Suddenly they hear a scrambling sound, and turn to see a pair of elves scampering away around a corner.

Run after the elves?
Go to page 13.

Leave the castle and explore the countryside?
Go to page 18.

See what's beyond the forbidding doorway?
Go to page 22.

"Quick—after them!" says Juranda. "Maybe they can tell us what's going on."

They dash after the elves, down the wide corridor of the castle. The elves are fast, but they soon enter a hallway which ends in a dead end. They turn, trapped, a look of terror in their eyes.

"Don't hurt Max," says the first elf, covering his eyes.

"Don't hurt Fred," says the other elf, trying to hide behind Max.

"Don't be silly," says Bivotar. "We don't want to hurt you. We just want to find out where we are and what's going on."

Max cautiously uncovers one eye. "Not going to hurt Max?"

Bivotar and Juranda shake their heads.

Fred peeks out from behind Max. "You've not been sent by Malifestro?"

"No," Juranda answers. "At least, I don't think so. Who's Malifestro?"

"Malifestro . . . ," begins Max.

" . . . powerful wizard. . . . ," Fred continues.

" . . . eats elves like us for breakfast," Max concludes.

Turn to page 14.

"That reminds me," says Bivotar. "I still haven't had breakfast."

The elves try to hide behind each other. "Don't eat us!" they whimper.

"I'm not going to eat you," Bivotar says gently. "Why are you two so frightened?"

"Evil times in Castle of Zork," says Max.

"Malifestro more powerful than anyone imagine," explains Fred.

"He lives in distant land where magic stronger than here in Land of Frobozz," adds Max.

"And now Syovar prisoner, no one can stop him," says Fred.

"Syovar! A prisoner?" says Juranda. "Where? Tell us more!"

Bit by bit, the elves reveal that the evil wizard Malifestro used a powerful spell to capture Syovar. Malifestro is holding Syovar for ransom in his own castle, far beyond the Flathead Mountains. The ransom includes a wealth of gold and jewels, half the land of the Kingdom of Zork, and ten thousand men to be enslaved by Malifestro.

The Knights of Frobozz, two thousand of

Turn to page 16.

the best soldiers of Zork, led by the noble Ellron, started out to rescue Syovar. Whether it was the awful power of Malifestro or the treacherous passes through the Flathead Mountains, none of the knights has been seen since.

Fear and despair have settled across the land. All order has vanished, and bands of thieves roam the highways and towns. It seems likely that Malifestro will easily conquer the entire kingdom.

"Most likely Malifestro will start here if he invades," says Max.

"So everyone has fled castle," says Fred.

"Except a few servants like us," adds Max.

"Too frightened to stay and too frightened to leave," concludes Fred.

"Oh, you poor things," says Juranda.

"Juranda, we have to do something. We must go and rescue Syovar."

"You can't!" gasps Fred.

"Wizard kill you," Max points out.

"Or eat you, like elves."

"Or turned into snails."

"Or boiled in oil."

"Or banished to snake pits."

Go to page 17.

"Or chained to Snow Monster of Snurth."
"Stay here in castle, with us."

Stay in the castle with the elves?
Go to page 25.

Attempt to rescue Syovar?
Go to page 28.

"We'll never catch those elves," says Bivotar. "Let's go outside. Maybe we'll find out what's going on."

They cross the creaking drawbridge over the castle moat and start down the wide dirt road across the grassy plain.

About half a mile from the castle, the road forks. One branch of the road leads down into a valley several miles away. They can see a number of small villages in the valley, surrounded by farmlands and sparse forests.

The other branch heads toward the distant mountains. The mountains are at least a day's journey away, and are so tall that their peaks are lost among the clouds.

"We're more likely to find people if we head toward the valley," says Juranda. Bivotar agrees.

They descend into the valley. At first it seems to be a cheery place, full of sparkling streams and abundant wildlife. However, as they get closer to the villages, the people they pass on the road are silent and glance distrustfully at the adventurers. Many of the farms are overgrown, and the farm buildings

Go to page 19.

are gutted by fire.

When they reach the nearest village, they head for the marketplace. It is deserted, except for an old misshapen woman, who is peeling a basketful of potatoes, and a hunchbacked man with an eyepatch. He is smoking a twisted pipe.

Turn to page 20.

"Ho! What have we here?" asks the old woman.

"We've just come from the castle," Juranda tells her. "We're looking for someone who can tell us where Syovar is."

"Alas," says the old woman. "He has been captured by Malifestro, an evil wizard from a neighboring land. Malifestro demands a mighty ransom for his return. Why do you seek Syovar?"

"Um, well, he's sort of our uncle," explains Bivotar, "and we heard he was in trouble."

The one-eyed man speaks for the first time. "You'd best forget your uncle if you know what's good for you. These are rough times even for them what minds their own business."

"Will the ransom be paid?" asks Juranda.

"Hard to say," says the old woman. "The kingdom isn't as wealthy as it used to be, what with all the thieves robbing people in the towns and burning the farms. And Malifestro also wants ten thousand men for slaves. There's certainly no one volunteering for that job."

Go to page 21.

"Why don't you two be gone?" says the one-eyed man. "There's nothing for you here."

Before they can answer, ten armed men ride into the marketplace, and one begins to bellow out a decree from the Mayor of the largest town in the kingdom. The Mayor is rounding up an army to attack Malifestro. Every able-bodied man in the village above the age of twelve is forced to enlist, including Bivotar. He and Juranda are terrified about being separated, but are powerless to prevent it.

That night, however, before Bivotar is hauled away to join the new army, the village is attacked by a large band of thieves. The village is burned to the ground, and everyone is killed.

THE END

If you stop here, your score is 0 out of a possible 10 points. But you probably deserve another chance.

Go to page 12 and try again.

"I'm not afraid of some bones or a few silly rats," says Juranda. "I'm going to see what's beyond that doorway."

"I'm coming too."

They enter the darkened room. When their eyes adjust, they realize that they are in an anteroom for a larger room beyond. An armed troll sits near the inner door. He must be much brighter than the average troll, for he speaks (though slowly and quite poorly).

"You, uh, you aren't supposed to, uh, come in here," the troll says.

"We were just looking around," says Juranda.

"Nice little kiddies," the troll says. He pats them on the head, nearly bashing their skulls.

"Ouch!" yells Juranda.

"Oh, uh, sorry. Too strong for my own good, mother used to say."

He gives them a friendly tap on the shoulder, breaking Bivotar's arm in two places.

"Oops. I sometimes, uh, forget my own, uh, my own strength. Now c'mon, go away before you get in, uh, in trouble."

Go to page 24.

He nudges them toward the door with his sword. Forgetting his own strength again, he accidentally slices them into pieces.

"Oops," says the troll.

THE END

If you stop here, your score is 0 out of a possible 10 points. But you probably deserve another chance.

Go to page 12 and try again.

Bivotar and Juranda stay in the castle with the two elves. They meet the other occupants of the castle: a grouchy cook, a pair of identical twin gnomes who work in the stables, a few dumb but loyal troll guards, and an ancient, totally deaf sorcerer who sits in his room all day, mumbling useless spells.

The days bring little news from the outside world. One day, while the elves and the adventurers are eating a skimpy dinner in the giant banquet hall, an enormous ball of fire appears in the center of the room. It fades to a cloud of smoke, and from this cloud steps a tall figure. He is old and thin, but his eyes burn with the vigor of youth.

"Malifestro!" Fred and Max shriek in unison, diving under the banquet table.

Malifestro waves his hand in front of his face, spreading a trail of sparks, and speaks in a voice that is both quiet and menacing.

"So, it is young Bivotar and Juranda, whose disquieting presence I felt from a land and a half away. The visitors from afar, who defeated the mighty Krill so easily. Had you come to me on your own terms, you might have posed

Turn to page 27.

a danger. As it is . . ."

He flicks a handful of sweet-smelling powder at them. Before they have a chance to react, they feel themselves slowly turning from flesh into stone. The last thing they hear is Malifestro saying, "This castle needed some new statuary, anyway."

THE END

If you stop here, your score is 1 out of a possible 10 points. But you probably deserve another chance.

Go to page 17 and try again.

"We must try to rescue Syovar," says Bivotar. The elves shake their heads in deep disbelief.

"Why don't you come with us?" asks Juranda. "You know the country better than we do, I'm sure."

"Oh, no. Can't," says Max, quickly.

"Not scared or anything," adds Fred.

"Don't like traveling that much," Max explains.

"But don't you think it's dangerous to wait around here?" asks Bivotar. "You said yourself that Malifestro will probably come straight here."

"Ohhh," wail the elves.

"Come on," urges Juranda. "It'll be fun."

"I guess we might as well," Max finally says.

"Yes, we'll be killed if we stay, and killed if we go, so we might as well keep you company," says Fred.

"Great!" says Juranda. "Let's get moving!"

"Wait. Wait!" says Max. "We should equip ourselves for the journey." He leads them to the forbidding doorway across from the castle's entrance.

Go to page 29.

"Are you sure we want to go in there?" asks Bivotar.

"Sure, no problem," said Fred. They enter, and find themselves in a small dark room leading to a brighter and larger room beyond. A heavily armed troll is sitting by the inner door.

"Hey, um, you aren't supposed to come in here, you know," the troll says, stumbling over his words.

"We're your replacements," says Max. "You can go now."

"About time. I've been here for, uh, three months now, and I'm sure starting to get tired and, uh, hungry." The troll lumbers away.

"Boy, trolls sure are dumb," says Juranda.

"Actually, he's one of the brighter ones," says Fred.

"Right. Most can't even talk," Max points out.

Upon entering the brightly lit room they see a small open trunk which holds various weapons—some knives, a sword, a mace, and some armor. Next to the trunk is a sack. They open it. It contains vials of potions and other magical devices.

Turn to page 31.

"If we take turns, we could probably carry the trunk or the sack, but definitely not both," Juranda announces.

"Let's take some stuff from each," suggests Bivotar.

"No!" shouts Max, "bad idea!"

"Right," agreeds Fred. "Mixing weapons and magic brings very bad luck."

"Then I say we should go with the weapons," states Bivotar.

"But, Biv—Ellron and the knights probably had plenty of weapons, and look what happened to them. I say we should take the magic."

Choose the sack of magic items?
Go to page 33.

Take the trunk of weapons?
Go to page 35.

Lugging the bulging sack, Bivotar, Juranda, Max, and Fred leave the castle.

"Malifestro's domain far beyond the Flathead Mountains," says Max, pointing at the distant towering peaks.

"It will take us days just to reach the mountains," says Bivotar with dismay, "and I still haven't had breakfast."

"Don't worry. Know shortcuts," says Fred.

"And here, have some waybread," says Max, reaching into his pack.

The road toward the mountains is wide and smooth. About an hour after leaving the castle, Max pricks his ears.

"I hear band of men approaching," he says.

"Oh no, oh no," says Fred. "I bet it's a pack of thieves."

"There's no good place to hide," says Juranda, glancing around.

"Let's look in the sack," suggests Bivotar. "There might be something we can use."

Max rummages around in the sack. "Aha!" he cries. "Invisibility cloak! Big enough for all four of us."

"Not reliable enough," says Fred. "Look,

Turn to page 34.

here's powder for casting friendliness spell."

"Are you crazy? Not strong enough!" The elves begin arguing wildly.

"Hurry!" shouts Juranda. "The voices are louder. They must be just around the bend!"

Would you use the invisibility cloak?
Go to page 36.

Would you cast the friendliness spell?
Go to page 38.

Carrying the small trunk of weapons, they approach the main gate of the castle.

"Let's get going," says Juranda, cheerfully.

The elves hesitate, glancing at each other and shaking.

"Not sure I want to go," says Max.

"It's all this talk of weapons," suggests Fred.

"Max terrible mountain climber," explains Max.

"Maybe we'll . . . go . . . next time," Fred adds.

"Right! Good luck! See you later!" The elves dash off into the heart of the castle.

"Too bad," says Bivotar. "They would have been interesting company."

They leave the castle, and head toward the distant mountains. About an hour later, they glimpse some men approaching on horseback. They are poorly dressed, and bellow a crude traveler's song.

"We can hide behind those rocks," Juranda points out.

"Why do we need to hide with all these weapons?" asks Bivotar.

Prepare to fight? Go to page 40.

Hide? Go to page 42.

Bivotar grabs the invisibility cloak from the sack and throws it around all four of them. At that moment, the band of men ride into view.

"Nothing happened!" says Juranda. "We're still visible!"

"Shhh," says Max. "We can see us, but they can't. Max hopes."

"Quiet," says Fred quietly. "Cloak doesn't stop noise."

Go to page 37.

The band of men, who indeed look like thieves, approaches them along the road. The cloak seems to be working. Just as they pass by, Fred lets loose a loud elvish sneeze.

The leader of the thieves pulls his mount to a stop. "Methinks I heard a sound," he says. He turns and stares straight at the spot where the elves and the two adventurers are standing.

Max holds a furry hand over Fred's nose. After a moment, the leader of the thieves shrugs and motions for the men to move along. A minute later, they have vanished from sight around a bend in the road.

"Whew, that was close," says Bivotar.

"Sorry," says Fred, wiping his nose.

"Fred allergic to thieves," Max explains.

Go to page 45.

As the elves continue to argue, the party of men appears around a bend in the road ahead. One cries. "Ho, men! Some travelers just standing and waiting to be robbed!" The men begin to gallop toward them.

"Quick, you idiots," shouts Juranda. "Cast the friendliness spell!"

Fred takes a vial of powder from the sack,

Go to page 39.

reads the label, and begins sprinkling the powder toward the approaching thieves.

"Chummo concordate vaxum," chants Fred. "Congenio jovio affabate!"

The thieves pull to a stop a few feet away.

"Why, look," says the leader of the thieves. "It's some cheerful elves and two charming adventurers."

"Ahh, let's leave 'em alone," says one of the thieves.

"Yeah, let's find a tavern," cries another.

"Would you care to join us for a round of drinks, good travelers?" asks the leader.

"Thank you, but we're already quite late," explains Juranda.

"Have a pleasant journey, then. Come men! Let us hasten to Elwood's Inn!" The thieves gallop off.

"I guess friendliness spells pretty strong after all," says Max.

Go to page 45.

Bivotar takes a mace and a shield from the trunk.

"Are you sure this is a good idea, Biv?"

"Don't worry. I saw someone use one of these in a movie once."

The men gallop toward them. They draw to a stop, and the leader of the men speaks.

"Hello, young travelers. Humblest apologies, but we're going to rob you. Have to, you know. It's our profession."

"Oh no you don't," shouts Bivotar. He gives a wild bellow, and hurls the mace toward the leader of the thieves. The mace flies off in the opposite direction and lands in a puddle about fifty feet away.

The leader shakes with laughter. "Search them," he orders.

The thieves search Bivotar and Juranda, removing the Ring of Zork and taking all of the weapons.

"What do we do with 'em now, boss?"

"Oh, just kill them."

THE END

If you stop here, your score is 2 out of a possible 10 points. But you probably deserve another chance.

Go to page 35 and try again.

They hide behind the rocks as the men ride into view. They definitely seem to be a pack of thieves. Bivotar and Juranda keep perfectly still until the thieves have vanished in the distance.

"Good thing we didn't try to fight them," admits Bivotar. "They looked pretty tough."

They continue journeying toward the mountains. As twilight falls, they come to a circular grove of trees near the side of the road. An enormous tree stump lies in the very center of the grove.

"This looks like a good spot to spend the night," says Juranda.

"Yes, we'll sleep in a tree," says Bivotar.

"But you hate climbing trees."

"I know, but there might be dangerous animals. Or more bands of thieves. Look, this tree here looks easy to climb, and it has some good nooks to sleep in."

* * *

The day dawns chilly and gray. Bivotar wakes Juranda and they climb down.

"What a night," groans Bivotar. "I hurt everywhere."

Turn to page 44.

"I feel fine," Juranda says. "Let's get going."

They continue to trudge toward the mountains. Bivotar complains about his stiff muscles and aching bones, and Juranda whistles a merry tune. The trunk of weapons seems heavier today, and they stop more frequently to rest. Finally, with the sun dropping in the west, they come to the base of the mountain range.

"Which way now?" asks Bivotar.

"I see a tiny cabin to the north."

"But there's some smoke from a campfire, off toward the south."

North?

Go to page 54.

South?

Go to page 56.

Bivotar, Juranda, and the elves continue their journey toward the mountains. As the sun begins sinking low, Juranda asks Fred, "Where are those shortcuts you mentioned? My feet hurt."

Fred peers down the road and points. "See that grove of trees down the road? Gigantic tree stump there. Magic very powerful. When we get to it, I'll show you shortcut."

In the grove, the trees form a rough circle around a large tree stump, at least ten feet across. The top of the stump is flat, almost like a large, round table.

"Fred remembers coming here in happier days," says Fred.

"Yes," Max agrees. "Syovar would bring everyone from castle out here for big feast. We would sit around tree stump eating dragon meat and hot-pepper sandwiches and garlic."

"Syovar entertained us. Performed feats of magic."

"And trolls battled for sport."

"Minstrels sang ballads about ancient Underground Empire of the Flatheads."

Turn to page 47.

The elves are silent for a moment.

Then Fred speaks. "Okay, everyone up on the tree stump." Fred reaches into the sack of magic items and pulls out a small pouch of tiny cakes.

"Eating these cakes will transport us directly to far side of Flathead Mountains," Fred explains.

"Oh no, Fred. Not those little cakes again. You tried them nine seasons ago, and they didn't work. You tried them five seasons ago and they didn't work. What makes you think cakes will work now?"

"Max, you boulderbrain. The cakes contain no magic themselves. That's why we had to come here; this tree trunk is a powerful source of magic. Those other times I just didn't have a powerful source of magic handy."

Max sighs and throws up his hands in resignation.

Fred hands everyone a cake, and begins reciting a spell: "Locomotis mova budgis transfio. Okay, eat cakes."

Everyone eats the cakes, which are hard and bitter.

Turn to page 48.

"I summon the power and magic of this stump," Fred chants. "Move us to the woods beyond the Flathead Mountains!"

The world blinks out for a moment. When it reappears, they have moved about three or four feet toward the Flathead Mountains. The sun is just touching the horizon.

"Max told you so," says Max.

"We moved three or four feet!" insists Fred.

"We should camp here for the night," says Juranda.

"Not safe outside at night," says Max.

"Many thieves around," agrees Fred.

"Anything in the sack for us to sleep on?" asks Bivotar.

Juranda looks inside. "Here's some kind of rug." She takes it out of the bag and unrolls it on the flat stump. The rug is square, about five feet on a side. As Juranda unrolls it, a red label falls out. It reads:

Frobozz Magic Carpet
Hello, Aviator!
To control your magic carpet,
just say "FLY" to fly and "LAND" to land.

Go to page 49.

"Oh good, oh good!" says Max. "Now can cross mountains before dark."

"I don't know," says Bivotar, looking skeptically at the carpet. "It seems kind of small."

"Plenty of room," says Fred.

"Elves small," Max points out.

Use the magic carpet?
Go to page 50.

Camp here tonight and continue by foot in the morning?
Go to page 80.

"Okay," says Bivotar, giving in. "Let's take the flying carpet."

"Oh boy, oh boy," says Max. "I haven't been on one of these in years!"

They all clamber onto the carpet, the elves elbowing each other for the best spot. When they are settled, Juranda yells "Fly!" The carpet begins to rise slowly from the tree stump.

"Yulp!" cries Fred, as his corner of the carpet sags. He grabs at Max, and both go tumbling over the side and fall to the grass below.

Without the weight of the elves, the magic carpet lurches upward. The two elves roll to their feet and run after the ascending carpet.

"Hey, Biv, wait for Max!"

"Juran, don't leave Fred behind!"

Bivotar looks down at them and tries to remember the proper command. "Halt!" he bellows. Nothing happens.

"Stop!" yells Juranda. Nothing happens.

"Return!" says Bivotar. "Down!" The carpet continues to fly.

"Where's that red label?" screams Juranda.

Turn to page 52.

By now, the carpet is flying briskly toward the Flathead Mountains. The grove of trees with the mighty tree stump is just a spot in the distance.

"Oh no, Biv, we've lost Max and Fred."

"Maybe they'll catch up," suggests Bivotar, without much conviction. "Meanwhile, we'd better figure out how to stop this thing." He continues looking for the label. The mountains are almost below them.

"What's that in your hand, Biv?" Juranda asks him.

"What, this? It's just that magic carpet label. . . ." He reddens. "Oh. Um. Hmmm. Well." He glances at the label. "Oh, of course! Land!"

The flying carpet turns and dives toward the ground. Faster and faster it falls. The ground rushes toward them. "We're going to crash!" Juranda yells.

Then, just before they hit the ground, the carpet slows down and lands with a gentle bump. They are close to the base of the Flathead Mountains.

"Whew," says Bivotar. "Some ride."

Go to page 53.

"We still haven't crossed the mountains," Juranda points out. "We'll have to give the carpet another try."

"Okay," Bivotar agrees. "Fly!"

The corners of the carpet flap a little, and then stop. Nothing else happens.

"Maybe we broke it," says Bivotar.

"It could just be used up, or something. Out of magic, the way a car can run out of gas."

"I guess we should have a look around, then."

"Look, there's a tiny cabin!"

"Hey, I can see smoke from a campfire. It doesn't look too far away!"

Would you go toward the cabin?
Go to page 54.

Would you go toward the campfire?
Go to page 56.

Bivotar and Juranda approach the cabin. It lies at the edge of a small stream which winds among the foothills here at the base of the mountains. The cheery glow of a fire can be seen through the window.

A narrow trail leads up into the mountains from here. In addition, a large cave opens into

Go to page 55.

the side of the mountain itself. A path leads downward into the cave.

"Which way do we go, Biv? The mountain path or the underground route?"

"Juran, it's going to be dark soon. Let's see if we could spend the night at the cabin there."

"It'll still be light for an hour. I keep thinking of Syovar hanging over those snakes. . . ."

"I'm exhausted. I think we'd make better time if we slept here and continued when we were fresher."

Take the mountain trail?
  Go to page 58.

Take the underground path?
  Go to page 61.

Ask for shelter at the cabin?
  Go to page 63.

Bivotar and Juranda head toward the smoking campfire. By the time they reach it, night has fallen. They stumble into the dark encampment and find themselves surrounded by a ragtag band of nomadic ogres. Ogres just love to eat people, and these ogres just happened to be getting ready for dinner.

THE END

If you stop here, your score is 2 out of a possible 10 points. But you probably deserve another chance.

Go back to page 31 and try again.

"You know, Biv," says Juranda as they begin climbing the mountain trail, "I've got this strange hunch that we're doing the wrong thing."

"That's funny. I've got the same feeling. But this is obviously the right way to go. We have no idea where that underground route goes."

The path gets steeper, and soon they are forced to abandon the equipment and supplies they brought from the castle. The temperature drops as they climb higher. The path leads along narrow ledges and between towering cliffs. The ascent is hard work, and they stop for frequent rests.

"It sure is cold," says Bivotar.

"I know, I know," says Juranda shivering.

Around midday, a light snow begins to fall, making the steep path very slippery.

"Let's stop for another rest," sasy Juranda, pointing to one of the few flat spots in sight.

"Sure," Bivotar agrees. "I hope we can get over the mountains before tonight. We'll freeze to death if we have to spend the night up here."

The snow begins falling more heavily.

Go to page 59.

"It sure is cold," says Juranda.

"It sure is cold," says Bivotar.

"Aaargrhgghzzhzz," says the seven-headed Snow Monster of Snurth, lumbering up behind them.

"Pardon me?" asks Juranda.

"I didn't say anything."

The leftmost head of the Snow Monster of

Turn to page 60.

Snurth takes a nibble off Juranda's shoulder, while its third-to-rightmost head delicately samples Bivotar's ear.

"Aaaiiieee," screams Juranda.

"Run!" yells Bivotar.

They begin running down the slippery mountain path, with the Snow Monster of Snurth right behind them. Unfortunately, all three of them—Bivotar, Juranda, and the Snow Monster—slip over a cliff and plunge thousands of feet to their death.

THE END

If you stop here, your score is 4 out of a possible 10 points. But you probably deserve another chance.

Go to page 55 and try again.

"I just remembered something!" Juranda says suddenly. "It was in my dream!"

"Right!" says Bivotar, remembering also. "Syovar said to take the underground route. He was trying to tell us the right way to go!"

The cave opening is tall and wide. Light pours in, showing that the trail leads downward. However, as they get further from the entrance, the light dims, and ahead it seems darker still.

Suddenly, the ground trembles from a far-off earthquake. With a deafening roar, the roof of the cave behind them crashes down! The cave opening is completely sealed off, leaving Bivotar and Juranda in total darkness and with no possibility of turning back. Sinister gurgling noises can be heard in the darkness around them.

"Quick!" says Bivotar frantically. "We need some light!"

Back at the castle, did you decide to take the sack of magical items?

If so, go to page 67.

Did you decide to take the trunk of weapons instead?

If so, go to page 70.

Bivotar and Juranda walk up to the door of the tiny cabin and knock timidly. After a moment, the door swings open, and standing before them is a man with gray, straggly hair. His deep eyes seem to soak the very strength from their bones.

"Excuse me," Bivotar begins, "we are . . ."

"I know who you are!" bellows the old man. "I have been watching you for a long time, a very long time." He motions for them to enter.

They enter the cabin. It is furnished only with a few stools and some soiled mats in one corner. Over the fire bubbles a pot of thin porridge. The old man directs them toward the stools and gives them each a bowl of porridge.

Turn to page 64.

"I am Vengrallior, an aged sorcerer from a long and ancient line of sorcerers. I was banished from the Land of Frobozz by Lord Dimwit Flathead—the very same Flathead whose name graces these mountains." He points dramatically at the mountains outside the window.

Bivotar takes a spoonful of porridge. It is bland and full of lumps. He tries to speak. "We are trying to find . . ."

"I know of your quest," Vengrallior interrupts. "My powers are not what they were when I was younger," he says. "In my heyday I could resurrect armies of the dead and create entire oceans overnight. However, I can still be of help to you."

"How?" asks Juranda.

"By feeding and sheltering you tonight, and perhaps by giving you some of the wisdom of my years." He stares deep into the heart of the fire, and speaks as if in a trance. "Turn not away from the one-eyed beast," he moans, "and pass ye through the gates of despair." Vengrallior falls back, exhausted by his prophecy.

Go to page 65.

"One-eyed beast?" asks Juranda. "Gates of despair? What does that mean? Why do you want to help us?"

"So many questions, little one. You must not be told too much, for only the meek and innocent may approach Malifestro without detection. Why do I help you? Because Malifestro is my mortal enemy. It is he who caused my exile, those many centuries ago, and I will never rest until he is destroyed." Vengrallior gives a wild laugh, and suddenly vanishes!

"Biv! Where'd he go?"

"Beats me. 'Turn not away from the one-eyed beast.' What do you suppose that means?"

"I don't know. And that part about passing through the gates of despair—any idea what that's about?"

"Nope. Let's get to sleep. We've still got a long way to go."

* * *

Juranda awakens first and rouses Bivotar. "C'mon, lazybones."

Bivotar stretches. "That was a good night's

Turn to page 66.

rest. Well, now for the mountains. The underground route looks creepy."

"But the mountain path looks steep and dangerous."

Take the mountain path?
Go to page 58.

Enter the cave?
Go to page 61.

"Look in the sack, Biv! Hurry!"

Bivotar reaches into the sack. "The only thing left is this big jar."

"What is it?"

The gurgling noises are much closer and seem to come from every direction.

"It's too dark to read the label. Let me open it." He opens the jar, and rays of sunlight stream outward, lighting the entire cave. All

Turn to page 68.

around, hideous creatures with long, slavering fangs howl with fear and dash away in every direction.

"Ugh," says Bivotar, shaking with fear and revulsion. "That was close."

Sunlight continues to stream from the jar, lighting every corner of the underground passage. Despite the brightness, the jar remains cool enough to hold.

Bivotar reads the label. " 'This jar contains one day's worth of Frobozz Magic Sunlight.' Well, let's get going—we only have one day of light."

They continue along the passage, which heads downward for a while and then levels off. Some portions of the passage are unfinished, the walls composed of rough, uneven rock. At other points, the passage has a smooth stone floor and tile walls. The walls in these areas look very old, and many tiles are missing.

At one point, the passage widens into a round room whose smooth walls are engraved with strange cryptic writing and pictures of giant ogres and ghostly shapes.

Go to page 69.

Several hours after leaving the round room, Bivotar and Juranda come to a point where the passage forks into four different tunnels. A young man wearing beautiful silken robes sits at the junction. He holds his head in his hands and moans.

"What a life," sobs the young man. "What a miserable life."

"Which way do we go?" Bivotar asks.

"We could try asking him," suggests Juranda.

"He's too depressing. Let's just pick one of the passages at random."

Ask the young man for directions?
Go to page 72.

Pick one of the passages at random?
Go to page 76.

"Biv! Isn't there a lamp in the trunk with the weapons?"

"Uh, no."

The gurgling noises are very close now. They seem to come from every side.

"I'm scared."

"Me, too."

The gurgling noises, it seems, are being made by a pack of hungry grues. The grue is

Go to page 71.

the most ferocious creature known to adventurers. It inhabits dark underground passages. Its long, sharp fangs are perfect for tearing into any kind of meat, although its favorite delicacy is adventurers. Its only fear is of light. Grues are always hungry.

Bivotar and Juranda, thanks to some extraordinary lack of luck, have wandered right into the middle of an entire lair of grues. Describing the results in further detail would probably prevent thousands of parents from buying this book for their innocent little kiddies (like you).

THE END

If you stop here, your score is 5 out of a possible 10 points. But you probably deserve another chance.

Go to page 31 and try again.

"Pardon me," says Juranda, approaching the sobbing young man.

"What?" he says, lifting his head and noticing them for the first time. He brightens a little. "Would you like to buy some shoes?"

"Huh?" she asks.

The young man looks crestfallen. "Of course not. No one does. I don't know why I even bother trying." He sighs deeply. "I suppose you're wondering who I am, and why I'm so depressed."

"Well, yes," admits Bivotar.

"I am Prince Melanchitis, heir apparent to the Throne of Kaldorn. I was once the richest man in the world, and I was about to wed Princess Despondia, the most beautiful maiden in the kingdom.

"My father, the King of Kaldorn, decided to help prepare me for the throne by putting me in charge of the Kaldorn Department of Revenue. I decided to raise taxes a bit, to show Dad that I was tough enough to be King. Unfortunately, I raised them a little too high. 110 per cent, to be exact. I never was very good at math," he adds, miserably.

Go to page 73.

"Anyway, the people revolted, killed my father, and exiled me here to this barren, underground world. Hungry and penniless, I decided to make ends meet by peddling magic shoes. I figured that everyone needs a few pairs of magic boots or slippers. But ever since this Malifestro episode began, business has been terrible. I haven't even sold a pair of magic shoelaces in months." The Prince of Kaldorn wipes a tear from his cheek.

"That's such a sad story," says Juranda.

"We're trying to find Malifestro and stop him," says Bivotar. "When we do, your business may pick up again. Could you tell us which tunnel to take?"

"Huh? Oh, it doesn't matter. They all go to the same place." The Prince thinks for a moment. "Let me give you a present for listening to a washed-up prince. Take these magic sneakers. I'll never sell them anyway. Here's a beautiful orange pair with purple stripes for the young lady, and a nice pink pair with green polka dots for the young man."

Thanking the Prince of Kaldorn for his gifts, Bivotar and Juranda head down one of

Turn to page 75.

the tunnels. Behind them, they hear the Prince sobbing again. "What a life. What a miserable life . . ."

Go to page 76.

As they head down one of the four passages, they notice that the light from the jar is a bit dimmer.

"We'd better hurry," comments Bivotar.

About ten minutes after leaving the junction, the four passages meet. They come to another junction. The four passages join here to form one main passage ahead.

On the ground is a glass bottle. Juranda examines it, then says: "According to the label,

Go to page 77.

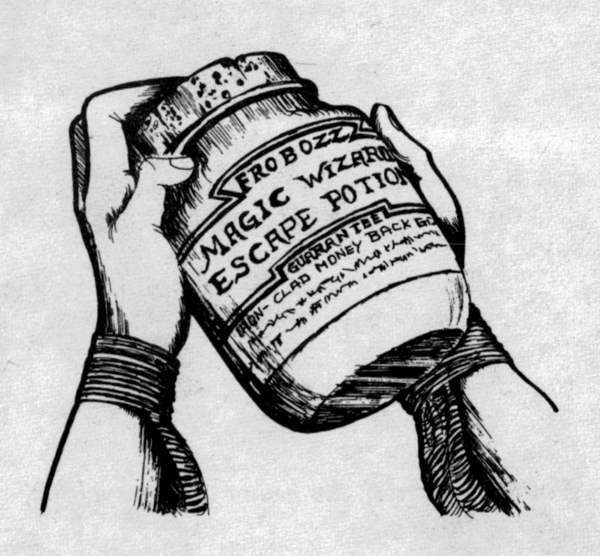

it contains Frobozz Magic Wizard Escape Potion, ideal for escaping from any wizard under any conditions. It comes with an iron-clad money-back guarantee."

"Let's hang onto it," says Bivotar, putting it into the sack. "Sounds as if it might come in handy."

Further along the passage they come to a heavy wooden door. It is over twenty feet tall. A massive metal doorknocker is just within reach. A mail slot has been cut through the door, about a foot high and four feet wide. Above the slot is a sign which reads:

Walter U. Smith
Cyclops

A side passage heads off to the left.

"I don't like the looks of that sign," Juranda says.

"That side passage there definitely looks sinister," says Bivotar.

Would you take the side passage?
Go to page 78.

Would you enter the home of the cyclops?
Go to page 82.

Avoiding the cyclops, Bivotar and Juranda take the side passage. It is very straight and the journey is uneventful at first.

Perhaps a mile beyond the cyclops' door, they turn a corner in the passage, and see a pack of hobgoblins gnawing on the carcass of some unfortunate animal. One of the hobgoblins spots them.

"Gurt-ham eato hicket thum!" the hobgoblin calls, pointing at the two adventurers. The hobgoblins begin trotting toward them, salivating heavily.

"We'd better turn back," suggests Bivotar.

"Not likely," says Juranda. "There are about ten more behind us."

The hobgoblins close in and began preparing their favorite dinner, adventurer stew.

THE END

If you stop here, your score is 6 out of a possible 10 points. But you probably deserve another chance.

Go to page 77 and try again.

After a lengthy argument, Bivotar convinces the elves to camp here for the night. They build a small campfire, and spread the magic carpet out on the flat top of the giant tree stump. As they sit around the campfire, the elves tell more stories of Syovar and life in the castle. The day has been long and hard, and soon everyone has fallen into a deep sleep.

During the night, a lone thief passing by spots the light from their dying fire. He quietly robs them, carefully slits their throats with his stiletto, and then slips silently away into the darkness.

THE END

If you stop here, your score is 3 out of a possible 10 points. But you probably deserve another chance.

Go to page 49 and try again.

"Juranda! Remember Vengrallior's prophecy?"

"Right! Turn not away from the one-eyed beast. A cyclops is a one-eyed beast."

"If Vengrallior said so, I guess it's safe." Bivotar walks up to the huge door and bangs the knocker. The noise echoes through the underground tunnels.

The door flies open, and a cyclops stands before them, roaring wildly. He is easily twenty feet tall, with rows of long, sharp teeth. He rubs his eye, which is half-closed. He looks a lot like a cyclops who has just been roused from a deep sleep.

The cyclops nudges them inside. He slams the door closed and bolts it securely.

"Yum. Yum. Breakfast." The cyclops begins setting his gigantic dining room table. "Very hungry. What a nice surprise."

"I don't like the looks of this," whispers Juranda.

"No other exits besides that door, and it looks pretty securely bolted."

"Um. Yum. Little tender breakfast people." The cyclops reaches into a cupboard and pulls

Go to page 83.

out salt and pepper shakers, each about three feet tall.

"Juran, we'd better think of something, quickly!"

"I've got an idea," Juranda says quietly. "He doesn't seem too bright." She raises her voice. "I think Odysseus should be here soon."

Turn to page 84.

The cyclops freezes, and his eye darts around the room.

"Oh, right," says Bivotar, catching on. "Odysseus ought to be here in about, uh, five minutes."

The cyclops shivers and drops a twenty-five-gallon jar of ketchup. "Odysseus? He blinded my father. Him coming here?"

"I think I hear him now," says Juranda. Drops of sweat begin pouring off the forehead of the cyclops.

"He's at the door!" shouts Bivotar. "He's coming in!"

The cyclops bellows with fear, and runs away from the door. He crashes through the far wall, leaving a cyclops-sized hole, and disappears from view.

"Good thinking, Juranda."

"Thanks, Bivotar. I'm glad we read Homer's *Odyssey* in school."

They climb through the cyclops-sized hole, and find themselves in a tunnel leading steeply downward. The tunnel soon becomes a long flight of wide marble stairs. At the bottom of the stairs is a wide doorway. Inscribed above

Go to page 85.

the portal are the words "Temple of Zork" and in smaller lettering "Joel Flathead, High Priest."

Bivotar and Juranda enter the temple. It has a high arched ceiling, and rows of stone benches. Cobwebs and dust cover everything.

"This place gives me creeps," says Juranda.

"Let's go up to the altar," says Bivotar.

They cross the temple and climb a few steps to the altar, where they find a heavy prayer book, a pair of candles, and a book of matches. The book is titled "Twenty-Two Favorite Exorcism Prayers of the Great Underground Empire."

"Let's take this stuff with us," says Bivotar.

"Why?" asks Juranda.

"I don't know. Just a hunch."

At the far end of the temple is another passage leading down. They follow it for several minutes and soon come to a small room with iron gates set into one wall. A hot wind blows through the gates, and beyond they can see flames and piles of bodies. The gates bear an inscription: "Abandon every hope, all ye who enter here."

Turn to page 86.

Opposite the gates, a forbidding staircase spirals downward. A foul-smelling draft comes from the stairway.

Attempt to pass through the gates?
Go to page 87.

Explore the spiral staircase instead?
Go to page 90.

"The second half of Vengrallior's prophecy!" says Bivotar.

" 'Pass through the gates of despair'! Good thing we ran into that old sorcerer. I never would have gone in there otherwise."

As they try to go through the gates, they are stopped by an unseen force. Invisible spirits laugh and jeer at their attempts to pass. From beyond the gate comes the wailing of thousands of lost souls.

"This is creepy, Biv. How can we get through?"

"We'll have to get rid of the spirits that are blocking our way."

"Good thing you brought that book of exorcisms from the temple."

Bivotar strikes a match and lights the two candles. Their flames flicker wildly, and a hush falls over the jeering wraiths. Bivotar flips open the book and reads one of the incantations. The spirits, acknowledging a power greater than theirs, scream with pain and flee. The room is suddenly silent.

Nervously, they enter the land beyond the gates. Walls of fire leap upward from the un-

Go to page 89.

seen depths below. Juranda points to a narrow ledge that winds upward, safely away from the flames. They follow the ledge, which eventually becomes a small tunnel, sloping upwards. The light from the jar is now definitely dimmer.

The grade of the tunnel becomes steeper, and its floor is now uneven and strewn with rubble. It becomes harder and harder to continue.

Did you get the magic sneakers from the Prince of Kaldorn?

If so, go to page 92.

If not, go to page 97.

They begin climbing down the spiral staircase. They continue downward for thousands of steps. At last, with no bottom in sight, they give up and turn around.

Up the stairs they go, spiralling around and around. Each step, each turn of the stairway, looks exactly alike. They begin to get worried.

Go to page 91.

"It didn't seem as if we went down this far," says Juranda.

"Maybe we missed the exit. Let's go a little farther, and then we'll turn around and try going down again."

They continue wandering up and down the stairway, but are unable to find the place where they entered. There doesn't seem to be any way out; the stairs seem to go on forever. Eventually, Bivotar and Juranda, tired and terrified, faint from hunger as their light slowly burns out.

THE END

If you stop here, your score is 7 out of a possible 10 points. But you probably deserve another chance.

Go to page 86 and try again.

"Let's put on the sneakers that the Prince gave us," says Bivotar. "It might make the going easier."

"Good idea," agrees Juranda.

They put on the sneakers, but before they have taken a step, a giant toad leaps out of the shadows behind them. It looks big enough to swallow both of them whole. The toad gives a deep croak, and its tongue lashes out toward them. It tries to wrap itself around Bivotar's leg, but he shakes himself free. The toad hops closer.

"Run, Biv! Run!" They begin running up the passage. Amazingly, each step seems to carry them many yards. Their feet barely seem to be touching the ground. They almost fly up the tunnel.

The giant toad leaps after them, croaking angrily. Its powerful hind legs propel it forward in long leaps, and its tongue lashes out toward them.

Ahead, a light appears at the end of the tunnel. Bivotar and Juranda soar toward the light with their long strides. Eventually, the giant toad falls behind, furious croaks echo-

Turn to page 94.

ing in the distance. The light from the jar sputters and dies.

They burst out of the tunnel into sunlight. Behind them are the mountains. Ahead of them is a forest of twisted trees. Rising above the treetops are the spires of an evil-looking castle.

"What took so long?" asks Fred, sitting on a rock next to Max.

"Max! Fred! How did you get here?" Juranda asks.

"Max used secret spell to summon mountain nymphs," says Max.

"Fred cast spell," says Fred.

"You cast spell and giant bat appears instead of mountain nymph," says Max, getting angry.

"Fred didn't summon bat," yells Fred. "Fred saved us from bat's lair on mountaintop!"

"By getting us into snow avalanche? You call that saving, you troll-brain?"

"A lot of help you were! You didn't kill a single one of the snow scorpions!"

"Max killed more than you!"

Go to page 95.

"You did not!"

"Max did!"

"Okay, okay," says Bivotar, trying to calm the elves. "We had a pretty exciting time, also. We ran into a cyclops, and a giant toad, and . . ."

"We also found this bottle of potion for escaping from wizards," Juranda interrupts.

"So what should we do now?" Bivotar asks.

"Malifestro's castle is there, within those woods," says Max, his voice quaking.

"Still not too late to turn back," suggests Fred.

"That forest does look pretty sinister," agrees Bivotar.

Try to return to the Castle of Zork?
Go to page 96.

Continue the quest?
Go to page 99.

Although it seems a shame to turn back after having come so far, Bivotar and Juranda agree to return to the Castle of Zork.

The trip back is very treacherous. The elves disappear during an attack by a pack of frost giants. Shortly thereafter, Bivotar accidentally triggers a magical underground anti-trespassing device, and brings several thousand tons of rock down on top of them.

THE END

If you stop here, your score is 6 out of a possible 10 points. But you probably deserve another chance.

Go to page 95 and try again.

"This is getting pretty steep," comments Juranda. "I wish we had something else to wear besides these stupid leather boots."

Suddenly, a giant toad leaps out of the shadows behind them. It hops toward them, its enormous mouth wide open.

"Run!" shouts Bivotar, heading up the passage. In the distance ahead, a tiny dot of light can be seen. Bivotar and Juranda try to run toward it, but trip on some rubble and fall to the ground.

In a moment, the giant toad is upon them. It wraps its long tongue around them and lifts them delicately into its gaping mouth.

THE END

If you stop here, your score is 8 out of a possible 10 points. But you probably deserve another chance.

Go to page 69 and try again.

"We're not turning back after we've come this far," says Juranda.

They enter the forest. Snakes slither by underfoot, and dark birds with long beaks hop from branch to branch. They move quickly, and soon arrive at the tall stone walls of Malifestro's castle.

"What are we going to do now?" asks Bivotar. "Knock on the door?"

"Knock on the door!?" scream the elves.

"Just a joke," says Bivotar.

"There are some vines growing up that wall," says Juranda, pointing to one of the towers. "We might be able to climb them."

"Wait! Fred has vision," says Fred.

"Oh, no, not again," says Max.

"Fred sees tower surrounded by vines," says Fred with his eyes closed.

"So what?" says Max. "So does Max."

"Fred sees black sphere in tower. Someone imprisoned inside."

"Who's imprisoned inside it?" asks Bivotar. "Syovar?"

Fred shrugs. "Fred cannot say. Vision gone."

Turn to page 101.

They carefully approach the tower wall. The vines are thick and securely affixed to the stone. The elves start climbing first, with Bivotar and Juranda right behind. The vines become thinner as they get farther from the ground. Just as it seems that they won't be able to climb any higher, they reach a small window.

The four of them crawl inside and find themselves in a small room lit only by the single window. A pentagram is inscribed upon the floor in the center of the room. Sitting near the window is a black crystal sphere, about two feet across.

"The black sphere!" exclaims Juranda. "Your vision was correct, Fred!"

"Max feels life force from within sphere," says Max, examining it.

"Malifestro must have Syovar imprisoned within that sphere!" says Bivotar. "How can we get him out?"

"Try putting sphere on pentagram," suggests Fred.

Bivotar puts the sphere on the pentagram. With a flash of smoke, a large demon appears,

Turn to page 103.

towering above them. The elves shriek and hide behind Bivotar and Juranda. The demon bares his fangs, and speaks in a voice that booms like rolling thunder.

"Hello, adventurers! Thank you for freeing me from my captivity! What's that behind you? Elves? I love the taste of tender elf meat!"

The elves grab each other, quaking with fear.

"And what's that you're carrying, young one? Is that a bottle of Frobozz Magic Wizard Escape Potion? Hmmm. Tell me, why have you come here? Why have you summoned me?"

"We have come to rescue our uncle, Syovar, from the evil wizard Malifestro," explains Bivotar.

"Then you come too late. Malifestro has already disposed of your uncle, and even now is preparing to invade the Kingdom of Zork."

"Syovar is dead?" says Juranda, stunned.

"I'm afraid so," says the demon. "But, just so your trip won't have been a complete waste of time, let me make you an offer. I'll grant

Turn to page 104.

any wish that is within my power to fulfill. All I ask for in return is that bottle of Wizard Escape Potion."

"That sounds reasonable," says Bivotar.

"Hey, wait!" says Max. "Potion could be only chance of getting out of here alive."

Would you hang on to the escape potion?
Go to page 105.

Would you strike a bargain with the demon?
Go to page 109.

"I guess that if Syovar is dead, our quest is over," says Bivotar.

"We've failed," adds Juranda. Her eyes fill with tears.

"Let's drink Wizard Escape Potion," says Max.

"Right," says Fred. "Sooner the better."

Bivotar shrugs. "We might as well save ourselves." He takes a gulp of the potion and passes the bottle around. The demon continues grinning. Juranda drinks the last of the potion.

After a moment, there is a loud pop, and a gnome appears. He is dressed in a three-piece suit, and carries a thick briefcase. He approaches the elves and the adventurers.

"I am a representative of the Frobozz Magic Wizard Escape Potion Company. I am here to insure that your escape is fast, safe, and legally correct. Now, what is your intended destination?"

"The castle of Syovar," says Bivotar.

The gnome gets a listing from his briefcase. "Hmmm. Can't find that on my list. Could you possibly mean the Castle of Zork?"

Turn to page 107.

"Yes, that's it," says Max. "Hurry!"

"Patience," says the gnome. "Ninety-five percent of all litigation is caused by undue haste. Now, I must have the name of the wizard you wish to escape from."

"Malifestro," says Juranda.

"Is that one 'L' or two?"

"One!" yells Fred.

"And your names?" asks the gnome, scribbling furiously on a legal pad.

Bivotar tells the gnome their names. The elves fidget nervously. The demon laughs at their discomfort.

"Now, you must sign these release forms, clearing the company from any future obligations other than the exact escape in question. You must sign all seven copies in the thirteen places indicated."

Suddenly, there is a huge puff of black smoke at the other end of the room. A tall figure wearing black, flowing robes steps from the cloud of smoke.

"It's Malifestro!" cry the elves, diving for cover.

"I'm afraid the guarantee is void without

Turn to page 108.

your signatures," says the gnome, disappearing with a pop.

Malifestro steps forward. The demon shrinks back in fear. The wizard points his wand at Bivotar, who turns into a mushroom. He casts a spell on Juranda, and she becomes a lizard. Malifestro then picks up the quaking elves, and carries them off toward his kitchen for a light snack.

THE END

If you stop here, your score is 8 out of a possible 10 points. But you probably deserve another chance.

Go to page 104 and try again.

"Maybe this demon can help us out," says Juranda. "Let's give him the escape potion."

"No!" says Fred.

"Give us escape potion instead!" says Max.

"Shut up, you two," says Bivotar. He asks the demon, "How can we trust you?"

"I will grant the request first," answers the demon, gesturing magnanimously.

"Okay," says Bivotar. "It's a deal."

"What are we going to ask for, Bivotar?"

"I'm not sure, Juranda. What do you think?"

Decide what you will ask the demon to do.
Once you have decided, turn to page 110.

Ask the demon to kill Malifestro?
Go to page 111.

Ask the demon to save you from the wizard and return you to safety?
Go to page 114.

Ask the demon for riches and treasure?
Go to page 116.

Ask the demon to try to bring Syovar back to life?
Go to page 118.

Ask the demon for something not listed above?
Go to page 125.

Bivotar says, "Demon! Kill the wizard! Kill Malifestro for us!"

The demon gulps. "Well, a promise is a promise." He disappears.

"Great idea, Biv!" says Juranda.

Suddenly, a tall man dressed in robes of the deepest black appears. He holds the demon by the scruff of his neck. The demon shrugs and says "Sorry, I tried."

The elves scream and try to hide in a corner. The robed figure steps toward the adventurers.

Turn to page 113.

"I am Malifestro," he says, "and you are an annoyance I have no time for." He conjures up an enormous fireball and flings it toward them. They are reduced to small piles of gray ash.

THE END

If you stop here, your score is 9 out of a possible 10 points. But you probably deserve another chance.

Go to page 109 and try again.

"Hey, demon," says Juranda. "Take us safely to Syovar's castle, and you may have the potion."

The demon nods at them, and immediately they find themselves in the throne room of the castle, minus the bottle of Wizard Escape Potion.

"Home," sighs Max.

"Safe again," says Fred.

"Relatively," adds Max.

Two days later, Malifestro and his servants of evil invade the land and enslave all the people in the kingdom.

THE END

If you stop here, your score is 9 out of a possible 10 points. But you probably deserve another chance.

Go to page 109 and try again.

"Demon! Give lots of jewels," shouts Max.

"And gold! Don't forget gold!" says Fred.

"Be right back," says the demon, vanishing.

"What a dumb thing to ask for!" says Bivotar.

"What are we going to do with jewels and gold?" asks Juranda.

"Jewels nice to look at," says Max.

"Gold always good to have," explains Fred.

The demon reappears, with a huge pile of jewels and gold pieces. "Here is your treasure," says the demon, "for all the good it will do you." He reaches down and takes the escape potion, drinks it, and vanishes.

"Oh boy, oh boy," says Max, grabbing handfuls of jewels.

"Great!" says Juranda. "We couldn't carry all that even if we did know how to get out of here."

Suddenly, a tall man wearing flowing black robes appears in the room.

"It's him!" screams Fred. "It's Malifestro!"

The elves burrow into the pile of treasure, their legs waving in the air. Malifestro raises one eyebrow ominously and says, "I was won-

Go to page 117.

dering where all my treasure went." He snaps his fingers, and the jewels disappear. He snaps his fingers again, and the gold disappears. He snaps his fingers again, and the elves disappear. He snaps his fingers again, and Bivotar and Juranda disappear.

He wipes his hands on his robe. "Good riddance. I hate kids," he mutters.

THE END

If you stop here, your score is 9 out of a possible 10 points. But you probably deserve another chance.

Go to page 109 and try again.

"Demon!" says Juranda. "Do you think that you could bring Syovar back to life, here?"

The demon frowns. "Hmmm . . . a most difficult request. I am not certain if even a Demon First Class like myself, with over seven hundred years of experience, can perform such a feat. However, I have promised, so I shall attempt to do as you ask. Also, if I am successful, then Syovar will be able to destroy Malifestro, which will repay that wizard for imprisoning me for three hundred years."

The demon chants complex spells, and draws intricate patterns in the air. Smoke pours from the ground before him. Sparks fly from his fingertips. Finally, the smoke clears, and Syovar is standing before them, looking slightly dazed.

"Juranda and Bivotar! You heard my call!" He embraces them affectionately. "And Max and Fred!" He pats the elves on their heads. They jump up and down with excitement.

"Sorry to break up this sweet reunion," says the demon, "but we did have a bargain." He coughs lightly.

Turn to page 120.

"Oh, right," says Bivotar. He hands the bottle of escape potion to the demon.

"Bye, everyone. Don't forget to write." The demon drinks the potion and disappears.

"The last thing I can remember is hanging over a snake pit," says Syovar. "Malifestro was there . . ." He trails off. "You had the demon bring me back to life! Frobs above, you've saved me again."

"We're still in Malifestro's castle," explains Juranda.

"And we've got to hurry!" says Bivotar. "The demon said that Malifestro is preparing to invade the kingdom."

Syovar chuckles. "Malifestro is a vain and boastful one. Before he killed me, he told me all his plans, how he would enslave the entire kingdom. I learned his strengths and weaknesses. He never dreamed I would live to use that knowledge."

"I must engage Malifestro in mortal combat," Syovar continues. "If I meet him in the throne room of his own castle, he will be unable to summon additional help. It would be just his magic against mine, his wits against mine."

Go to page 121.

"Be careful!" warns Max.

"Right," chimes Fred. "Getting killed twice in same week very unhealthy."

Syovar nods solemnly at them, and claps his hands. Bivotar, Juranda, and the elves find themselves on a balcony overlooking the throne room. Syovar stands below, in the center of the room. As they watch, Malifestro appears in a cloud of acrid smoke.

"How many times must I kill you, Syovar?" asks the evil wizard.

"It's my turn now," Syovar answers. He waves his arm, and turns himself into a ferocious mountain lion. He lunges at Malifestro, who turns himself into a raging wall of fire.

Syovar leaps back with a roar, and suddenly the lion is gone, replaced by a wave of water rushing toward the fire. The fire vanishes, and in its place comes a howling wind of cold air. It blows over the water, which is pushed back and slowly starts to freeze. The water becomes a sheet of ice, as the wind continues to howl around the throne room.

"Oh no, oh no," wails Max. "Malifestro is freezing him."

Turn to page 123.

Before their eyes, the sheet of ice begins to change shape, flowing outwards. Its edges curl upwards, meeting to form a gigantic, translucent sphere around the whirlwind. The sphere shrinks and shrinks, and a moment later, Syovar stands below them, holding a crystal sphere just like the one that imprisoned the demon. The elves let loose a wild cheer of delight.

Syovar waves his arm again, and suddenly they are back in their own castle. Syovar, exhausted from his battle, leaves the elves to look after Bivotar and Juranda while he retires for the night.

By the next morning, word has spread of Malifestro's defeat. Throngs begin gathering on the meadow outside the castle.

Syovar takes Bivotar and Juranda to a balcony overlooking the cheering crowd. Max and Fred come along as well.

"Hail, Syovar!" yells the crowd. "Long live the king!"

"Thank you for your fine welcome!" Syovar calls out to them. "But let me introduce the two heroes who risked their lives to save me.

Turn to page 124.

Bivotar the Brave, and Juranda the Dauntless!" The people cheer wildly.

"But we couldn't have done it without Max and Fred," Bivotar yells.

"The two bravest elves in the world," adds Juranda.

The two elves try to look modest, but don't quite succeed.

Syovar embraces the two adventurers and whispers, "Better say farewell to the elves."

"Goodbye, Max," says Bivotar, wiping a tear from his cheek.

"I'm going to miss you, Fred," Juranda says, sniffling.

"Max doesn't want you to leave," says Max.

"Fred wants you to stay, too," says Fred.

"We have to go home," explains Bivotar. "But we'll be back."

They begin to feel dizzy. Their heads spin, and the world becomes a blur.

Go to page 126.

Before they have a chance to ask the demon for anything, Malifestro appears in the room. He orders the demon back into his spherical prison. Then, with a wave of his hand, he sends Max, Fred, Bivotar, and Juranda to similar prisons of their own.

THE END

If you stop here, your score is 9 out of a possible 10 points. But you probably deserve another chance.

Go to page 109 and try again.

When their heads stop spinning, they see that they are back in Bill's bedroom. June is wearing her normal clothes and Bill is back in his pajamas, clutching the Ring of Zork in one hand. He puts the ring back in the top drawer of his bureau.

"Bill!" shouts Bill's mother from down the hall. "Are you awake?"

"Yes, Mom!" Bill answers.

"Breakfast is almost ready!" she calls.

"Okay!" says Bill, smiling broadly.

June darts over to Bill's window to climb out. She looks at Bill. "I'm going home. I'll see you later." She lowers her voice. "Let's not stay away so long this time."

"Okay!" says Bill, smiling broadly.

THE END

Your score is 10 points out of a possible 10 points. Congratulations! You would make a fine adventurer.

Bivotars and Jurandas everywhere, your adventures have just begun!

If you've been brave and clever and lucky enough to get this far in the book, you may be ready for ZORK computer games from Infocom.

You'll find more excitement behind the magic door to ZORK than you'll ever find in any arcade. Infocom makes three ZORK games in all, as well as thrilling mysteries like DEADLINE™ and The WITNESS,™ and science fiction games like STARCROSS,™ SUSPENDED,™ and PLANETFALL.™

You can get Infocom games at just about any computer store. We make them for all kinds of computers: Apple II, Atari, Commodore 64, CP/M 8," DEC Rainbow, DEC RT-11, IBM Personal Computer, NEC APC, NEC PC-8000, Osborne, TI Professional, TRS-80 Model I, and TRS-80 Model III. Be sure to buy the specially marked Infocom game that's right for your computer. And happy adventuring!

The next dimension.